Heads the Porridge

Sean Taylor
Illustrated by Carla Daly

RIGBY

Chapter 1

Anna and Benni had a small farm in the hills. They had one brown cow, some hens, a sheep, a goat, and a big field of hay. They lived in a little wooden house in the shelter of a grassy mound.

One morning, Benni sat down on his old rocking chair and sighed.

"Why are you huffing and puffing?" Anna asked.

"I'm tired," said Benni, "and I've got to cut the hay."

"You're just lazy!" said Anna.

Benni frowned. "You'd complain too, if you had to do what I do!" he said.

"Are you sure?" asked Anna.

"Oh, yes. As sure as a man can be!" said Benni. "I do more work in one day than you do in three."

"Well, if that's what you think," said Anna, "then why don't I cut the hay? You can stay here and do the things that I usually do."

"All right," said Benni.

"You can start by pouring the tea," said Anna.

"What do I have to do then?" asked Anna.

"Cut all the hay in the field," said Benni. "And I suppose all I have to do is rock the baby and make the bed?"

"That's right," said Anna. "And feed the sheep, and milk the goat, and clean out the chicken coop, and sweep the floor, and beat the rug, and chop the wood, and wash the sheets, and make the fire, and cook the porridge, and take the brown cow down to the grassy field."

Anna set off for the hayfield, and Benni sat down with a smile. "Well, this will be a fine day," he said. "Those chores won't take long."

He stretched his legs and looked around the room. "I might just drink another quick cup of tea," he thought. He drank his tea and sighed happily.

"Those chores won't take long. They won't take long at all," he said to himself. "Maybe I'll have a small cheese sandwich."

He started his sandwich and fell asleep by the warm fire.

An hour later he woke up. "Well," he yawned, "I'd better get those chores done."

So, he made the bed, and rocked the baby, and put the food for the sheep in a sack by the door.

Then he found the broom and swept the floor.

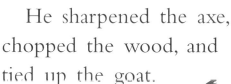

He sharpened the axe, chopped the wood, and tied up the goat.

He milked the goat, took the milk bucket indoors, and put the sheets in the washtub.

Then he took the rug outside
and started to beat it.

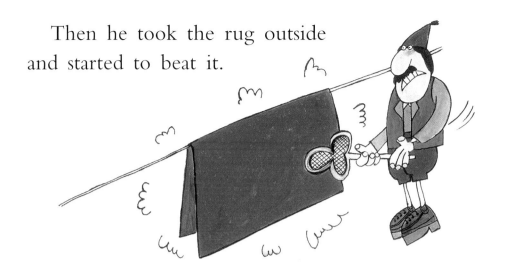

All this hard work was making him thirsty!
"I'll just go and get a cup of apple cider,"
thought Benni.

Benni went down to the cellar. The apple cider was in a large barrel. Benni put his cup under the tap and turned it on when suddenly . . .

Benni rushed back upstairs.

The sheep had come in through the open door and was standing in the kitchen. It had knocked the milk all over the floor.

Benni splashed through the milk and herded the sheep out of the door.

Benni was mopping up the mess when he heard a strange swooshing sound from downstairs.

"What could that be?" he thought. Benni hurried back down to the cellar and . . .

He saw that he had left the tap running.
He was up to his ankles in apple cider.
Just then, the baby started to scream, so he
rushed upstairs again.

Benni rocked the baby and washed the sheets in the washtub. Then he scrubbed the floor and cleaned out the chicken coop.

Then he hung out the sheets, and at that second . . .

it started
to rain!

Benni ran inside and dropped into his old rocking chair. "I'm so tired!" he thought. "I'll just take a little nap."

But when he saw the time he was so surprised that he almost fell off his chair.

Anna would be back any minute!

Chapter 2

Benni had just five minutes to make the porridge and take the brown cow down to the grassy field.

"Anna won't be at all happy if these chores aren't done!" he said to himself.

So he found the oats, stoked the fire, and put the porridge in the pot. Then he stopped. How was he going to take the brown cow down to the grassy field, *and* stir the porridge at the same time?

He rubbed his chin and stared into the fire.

Suddenly, he remembered the grassy mound behind the house. The cow could graze there.

He rushed outside, tied a rope around
the cow's leg, and took her up onto the
grassy mound.

Then he dropped the rope down
the chimney.

He ran back to the fireplace, and tied the
other end of the rope around his ankle.

"Now the brown cow can't run off," he
said to himself, "and the porridge will still be
ready on time."

However, the brown cow had never eaten on the grassy mound before. She was used to the grassy field, which was long and flat. There she would walk and eat, walk and eat, and she never bothered to look where she was going.

So now she just kept on walking and kept on eating. Soon, she had plodded onto the roof of the house and was eating the grass that grew in the gutters.

Benni was so busy stirring the porridge that he didn't notice the rope disappearing up the chimney.

The brown cow kept walking across the roof, and when she came to the edge, she fell off!

The rope yanked Benni by the ankle and . . .

whoops!

Benni went flying up the chimney!

At that moment, Anna came back from the hayfield. She saw the sheets hanging in the rain and the brown cow hanging from the roof.

"Benni!" she yelled, bursting into the house. All she could see was a pot of porridge bubbling over the fire. She couldn't imagine where Benni was or why he had hung the brown cow from the roof.

"MOOOOOOOOOOOOOOOO!!!"

complained the brown cow.

Anna rushed out, cut the rope, and . . .

well, you can guess what happened next!

"**MOO!**" cried the cow, as she landed back on the ground.

"**WHAAAAAAAAAAAAAARGH!**" screamed Benni as he fell down the chimney and headfirst into the porridge!

Anna laughed until she cried.

"Tomorrow I'm going to cut the hay!" said Benni, trying to scrape porridge out of his hair.

Anna looked at him, wiping the tears from her eyes. "Are you sure?" she asked.

"Oh, yes," said Benni. "As sure as a man can be!"